The Almost Awful Play

by Patricia Reilly Giff

illustrated by Susanna Natti

Troll Associates

PUFFIN BOOKS
A Division of Penguin Books USA Inc.
375 Hudson Street, New York, New York 10014
Penguin Books Ltd, Harmondsworth, Middlesex, England
Penguin Books Australia Ltd, Ringwood, Victoria, Australia
Penguin Books Canada Limited, 2801 John Street, Markham, Ontario, Canada L3R 1B4
Penguin Books (N.Z.) Ltd, 182–190 Wairau Road, Auckland 10, New Zealand
Reprinted 1986

First published by Viking Penguin Inc. 1984
Published in Picture Puffins 1985

Text copyright © Patricia Reilly Giff, 1984
Illustrations copyright © Susanna Natti, 1984
All rights reserved

Library of Congress Cataloging in Publication Data
Giff, Patricia Reilly.   The almost awful play.
Summary: Second-grader Ronald Morgan inadvertently
turns a failing class play into a success.
    1. Children's stories, American.   [1. Schools—
Fiction.   2. Plays—Fiction]   I. Natti, Susanna, ill.   II. Title.
PZ7.G3626Al   1985   [E]   84-17922   ISBN 0-14-050530-X

10   9   8   7   6   5   4   3   2

Printed in the U.S.A.

For Michael
John
and
Mari-joy
P.R.G.

With love to
Lydia Eeva
S.N.

"I have a surprise," Miss Tyler said.
"Is it a party," I asked,
"with chocolate cake and ice cream?"
"No, Ronald Morgan, it's a play.
We'll do it for the whole school."
All the children cheered.

We marched into the auditorium
to see the stage.
Miss Tyler said, "The name of the play is
The Darkest Dungeon."
She looked around.
"First we need a princess."
"Me, me!" yelled Rosemary.
"I look like a princess."
Miss Tyler nodded.

"We need a witch, too."
I raised my hand and so did Jan.
Jan made a scary, awful face.
"Jan's the witch," I said.
"You're right," said Miss Tyler.

"Maybe I could be the prince," I said,
and poked my best friend, Michael.
Rosemary asked, "Do you think you look
like a prince, Ronald Morgan?"
I thought for a minute.
"Maybe I could be the curtain puller."

But Michael wanted to pull the curtain,
and so did Alice and Billy.
Miss Tyler let everyone try.
The ropes were heavy.
Michael and Alice could hardly pull them.
Jan put a spell on me
and I tripped on the rope.
Billy pulled the best.
The curtain whooshed across the stage.
Miss Tyler said, "Perfect pulling, Billy."

"I'm looking for a prince," Miss Tyler said.

"Michael will be fine.

And, Ronald, you can be the cat."

"Meow," I said in a scared voice.

Everyone had something to do.
Alice and Jimmy drew posters,
and Jan and I fixed up her hat.

But Alice asked, "Who ever heard of
a pink witch?"
And Rosemary said, "I needed that glitter
for my crown."

"Don't worry," I said. "I saved some.
I'll help you pour it on."
But the bottle spilled,
and Rosemary cried
because Jan's witch hat had more glitter
than the crown.

Then Michael and I made a cat mask.
It was furry and black with whiskers.
"That's a neat mask," Jimmy said.
But Billy said, "You forgot to make the eyes."

Quickly I poked in two holes.
"Oh, no," Jan said.
"One eye is bigger than the other."
Now all the kids call me Winky.

Michael and I made the dungeon,
all scary with bars and chains.
I put lots of glue on the bars.

But the dungeon was a little crooked,
and Rosemary said, "What can you expect
from a cat?"

Then we started to practice.

I curled up near Rosemary

and smoothed out my long black tail.

"Watch out, Winky," Rosemary said.

"You're getting fur on my princess dress."

I crawled over a little to get out of the way.

Miss Tyler clapped her hands.

"Watch out, Ronald Morgan," she said.

"Don't fall off the stage."

Jan practiced putting Michael in the dungeon.
I was the good cat who gave him the key.
I liked the end part best
when Michael unlocked the dungeon.
"Princess, you are saved!" he'd shout.
Then we'd all line up and sing.

At last it was the day of the play.
I put on my cat mask
and peeked out of the curtain.
Everyone was there.

Quickly I ran to my place.
Billy pulled the curtain open
and all the children clapped.
Tom, the announcer, said,
"It's time for *The Darkest Dungeon*."
Then Jan said, "Ha, ha, ha,"
in a mean witch voice.
She waved her wand and
Rosemary fell on the floor.
I said a sad meow
because the princess was under a spell.

Michael, the prince, came out

but he didn't say anything.

He kept twirling the feather on his hat.

"I am the prince," I whispered,

to help him out.

"Sh," Rosemary said, "you're mixing us up."

Everybody laughed.

"I will save you, Princess," Michael said
in a little voice.
"Ha, ha, ha," Jan said.
She took Michael by the arm
and locked him in the dungeon.
I said my second meow.
This time it was a worried one.

It was time to get the key.

I said my brave meow and

sneaked the key out of the witch's pocket.

Just as I was giving the key to Michael,

my mask slipped.

I leaned on the dungeon and put

my fingers in the mask holes

so I could see.

The dungeon started to wobble.

It was wobbling a lot.

"Meow!" I said in my watch-out voice.

But it was too late.

The dungeon crashed.

"Some cat you are," Rosemary said.

"This is an awful play."

Everyone was waiting.

Someone had to save the princess.

I took off my mask

and grabbed Rosemary's hand.

"I'm really a prince, too," I said.

"Princess, you are saved!"

Then we all started to sing.

Miss Tyler told Billy
to close the curtain.
I forgot to step back
and I got caught outside.
Miss Tyler came outside, too.
"We have a new star," she said.
"Ronald Morgan!"
Everybody clapped.

Miss Tyler smiled. "Now it's time
for chocolate cake and ice cream."
Then I said my last meow.
This time it was a happy one.